For Jameson

Fox likes to talk stocks.

Fox likes when companies are compliant with SOX (Sarbanes-Oxley Act).

Fox likes when
P/E Ratios (Price-
to-Earnings) are
low.

Fox likes when her investments grow.

Fox likes to save her dimes.

Fox likes when her net worth climbs.

Fox likes to invest
in her 401K.

Fox likes the thought of retiring one day.

Fox likes to analyze economic trends.

Fox likes to discuss these with friends.

Fox likes to track the Dow (Dow Jones Industrial).

Fox likes when
a company is
a cash cow.

Fox likes when the deal is right.

Fox likes when she can finally call it a night.

CPSIA information can be obtained
at www.ICGtesting.com
Printed in the USA
BVHW011402020620
580743BV00003B/7